1.25

D0168356

Angela Anaconda ™

Pet Peeves

POCKET
BOOKS

CONTENTS

HARD TO SWALLOW

CHAPTER 1

Did you ever think something was going to turn out one way, then it turns out another? It happens all the time to me, Angela Anaconda. Especially on days that I think are going to be perfect, like the day I am going to tell you about. First of all, it was a Saturday, which means no school. Second of all, it was a day that I was going to be hanging out with my friends, including my best non-human friend, my dog King, at doggie obedience class. And third, and best of all, my parents were going to be picking up my

Grandma Lou at the airport.

She was coming over from her house in Florida to stay with us. Some Grandmas are old and boring and always tired, but not my Grandma Lou. We do exciting and interesting stuff when we visit her, such as race her motorboat around the swamps chasing after alligators. So you can understand why I couldn't wait to see her.

But still, King and I were also looking forward to our day together at the Please Re-leash Me Obedience School. King liked to see all the other dogs as much as I liked seeing all my friends. And there I was, waiting outside the school to see

which one of my friends and their pets would show up first when things started to go wrong. Very wrong.

"I know, people, I know. It was totally unnecessary for me to come," said a voice that was too horrible to be true. "I just thought that my perfectly trained and obedient, pure bred French poodle could provide a positive role model for the lesser breeds."

Nanette Manoir? And I thought I was going to be spending the day with my friends, not my most mortal enemy, who not only is nasty to me but to my dog King as well.

"Why, hello, King," said Ms Nit. "Dine in any good garbage cans lately?"

She would have to come along just as King has found a perfectly good Chinese take-away that someone had thrown out. So what if the carton was stuck to her nose and the chow mein was dripping off her fur? I'm sure it was perfectly good food, or King would not have been eating it. Nanette Manoir might be too unsmart to know it, but King happens to be a very intelligent dog.

After Ms Yamagachi, our special doggie behaviour instructor, had yelled at Gordy Rhinehart and his little dog,

Fabio, for being thirty-seven seconds late, Nanette had to pipe up with her ideas for what activity we should do, just like she does with Mrs Brinks in our real school.

"Excusez-moi, Ms Yamagachi," she said in her un-French French. "But I was hoping we could start with sitting, seeing as there are so many dogs who still have trouble with this simplest of commands. Unlike my Oo-La-La, of course."

Couldn't you just throw up? I could have and so could Gina Lash (who does not have a dog, but a turtle named Sheldon and only comes to doggie obedience school because she likes the treats), but not Ms Yamagachi. Even though she is strict with everyone and no one is her teacher's pet, for some reason she acted just like Mrs Brinks on this occasion and let Nanette tell her what to do.

"Excellent suggestion!" said Ms Yamagachi. "One, two, three, sit!"

At that, all Gordy and Fabio did was shake. They were still scared from being yelled at. Pious, Josephine Praline's dog, knelt down like it was saying its prayers.

"Come on, King, you know this one," I said to King, trying not to let anyone else hear me. For some reason King did not feel very obedient and I was trying to push her butt down. But, of course, Oo-La-blah sat right down, even her posture was perfect. Then Ms Yamagachi, who likes to keep things moving along, was ready for us to try the next command.

"One, two, three, ROLL OVER!" she shouted. Ms Yamagachi is a very busy person and she does not like to waste any time, not even thirty-seven seconds, so I was really worried when King would not do that trick either. She began to do it, but then she started scratching her back on the floor and never got up on her feet again. Oo-La-La, on the other hand, was rolling over and over

and over again like a little circus dog, which made King look even worse.

"Your mongrel simply doesn't have that certain *je ne say croissant*, which is French for: 'My dog is so much better than yours!'" said guess who in her un-French French. And I could not think of anything more annoying, until Nanette asked Ms Yamagachi if she could demonstrate a special trick that she had taught Oo-La-La.

And instead of yelling at Ninnie-Poo for wasting time, which is what Ms Yamagachi normally would do, she said, "Okey-dokey, but make it snappy!"

"Un, deux, trois KISSES!" squealed the revolting one, and Oo-La-La jumped into her arms and gave her a big wet kiss on the mouth! I probably don't have to tell you, I almost threw up.

"Gross," I said to Gina Lash. "Doesn't Oo-La-La know how many butts those lips have kissed?"

Chapter 2

On the way home, Gina Lash and I were trying to get King to stop pulling us around by the leash and walk like a normal dog. As you know, King is my absolutely best non-human friend in the world, but there are times when I wish she would just listen to me and do what I wanted.

"She's just asserting her independence," said Gina Lash, as she nibbled on some of the doggy treats. "King's a free spirit, with her own unique set of talents and abilities."

Good old Gina Lash, always ready to see the best in everyone, even when King does disgusting things like make us stop so she can sniff the fire hydrant.

"Hello, Angela," said a voice, which is too disgusting to describe. "Having trouble with your non-pedigreed pet again?"

And prancing beside Little Nin, still acting like he was part of the circus, was teeny tiny Oo-La-La, the teacher's pet of the dog world.

"My Oo-La-La," said the Nannoying one, "is so well-trained, he doesn't even need a leash. And unlike some dogs I could mention, he would never run away."

Wasn't she finished bragging yet? Then, thank goodness, they headed down another street.

"It would serve her right if he did run away," I said to Gina Lash. Gina was just about to agree with me, when she realised that her bag of dog biscuits had a hole in the bottom and most of her liver-icious treats had slowly been dropping out and making a trail behind us.

"Next time I'm double-bagging these," said Gina Lash. And just as we turned to see how many treats had fallen out of the bag behind us, we saw something that we never thought we would see.

Oo-La-La, Ninnie-Poo's perfect little un-French French poodle, who according to her, would never run away, was all alone behind us, eating up all the treats! This was just too good to ignore and I had an idea.

Chapter 3

"Now, what?" asked Gina Lash a few minutes later, as she dumped the rest of her dog biscuits out for Oo-La-La. We were in my backyard, where we had secretly tied up Oo-La-La under the tree.

"Now we watch the fun," I said. First of all, let me tell you that we did not tie Oo-La-La up very tightly. We just wanted to make sure he stayed in my yard. Second of all, my plan was to keep him just for a few hours until Ninky-Wink gave up and admitted that her perfect pooch had run away from her. Third of all, he really did love Gina Lash's doggie treats and did not mind one bit being away from his dog-training, baloney-headed mistress, who made him do horrible things like roll over and kiss her on the lips.

"Let's take a little walk past Nanette Manoir's house," I said to Gina Lash.

And we were just in time, too. Nin the Pin was on her

front steps calling, "Oo-La-La, time to frost your highlights!" And she could not believe it when her little slave dog did not do what she said.

"Oo-La-La? Where are you?" she called.

"What's the matter, Nanette?" I asked, as if I didn't know anything. "Don't tell me Oo-La-La got out!"

"He must have had an important appointment," said the huffy one, not letting her guard down. "But I'm not worried. A dog of Oo-La-La's superior breeding can always be counted on to come home. It's only mutts from inferior homes, like King, who run away." Then she stormed back into her house.

"Am I watching the fun yet?" asked Gina Lash. And to tell you the truth, that wasn't so fun. Who wanted to see Nanette or her pipsqueak pup one more minute anyway?

Chapter 4

So Gina Lash and I went back to my house to let Oo-La-Blah go. As we arrived, we saw my parents' car parked out front and I remembered the best part of the day.

"Hey! My Grandma Lou is here!" I yelled, and Gina Lash and I forgot all about Oo-La-La and we ran into the house.

"That my little Angie-Pangie?" yelled Grandma Lou. "And hi-dee-ho to you, Gina Lash! You two come here and give Granny a big old hug!"

After she had hugged both me and Gina Lash, Grandma Lou gave us each these great alligator-shaped hats shaped like alligators.

"It's just like the real thing!" I said.

"Aw, that's nothin'," said Grandma Lou. "Wait'll you meet ma pal, Barney."

"You've brought a friend?" I asked. Any friend of Grandma Lou's was sure to be as fun and interesting as her.

"Yep, he's in the backyard!" said Grandma Lou. "He ain't exactly what you'd call 'housebroken' yet."

"Out in the swamp, not everyone has indoor plumbing," I told Gina Lash.

"No, Angel-fish," my dad laughed. "Barney is Grandma Lou's pet alligator"

What did he say? A pet alligator, in our yard?

"Fact, when I went out to feed him, I found him chewin' on this," said Grandma Lou, as she handed me a certain poofy poodle's rhinestone collar. "Almost lost yourself a pretty fancy necklace there, kiddo."

"Wash our hands for dinner?" said Gina Lash, who would never miss a meal for any reason, even a serious reason like this one.

So then we sat down to the longest dinner of my life, a dinner that should have been a happy occasion with my favourite grandma who had just given me a new hat, but everything just kept reminding me of what must have happened to poor little Oo-La-La.

"You eatin' that dog?" asked my brother Mark, as he pointed to the last hot dog in the dish.

"Heck, you boys eat faster than my 'gator, Barney!" laughed Grandma Lou. "I'll swear that little fellow'll eat anything that ain't chained down."

"And some things that are," I said to myself, as I looked at Oo-La-La's empty collar. It was sparkling and one sparkle of light coming off it almost looked like a sparkle off a giant alligator's tooth.

Then I saw the big teeth of Barney the alligator in a hospital operating room. There I was, a famous doctor ready to perform an operation together with my trusty nurse, Gina Lash. Ninky-Wink would be there too, shaking her baloney curls and begging me to save the day.

"Doctor! Doctor! This giant pile of walking shoe leather has swallowed my precious poodle, Oo-La-La!" she will whine.

"Step aside, oh useless one," I will tell her, as I shove her out of the way. Nurse Gina brings in an X-ray machine and I turn it on. Sure enough, there in the belly of the beast is the little puffy poofball, Oo-La-La, doing all his poofy, puffy tricks.

"Please, oh great and wonderful Doctor Anaconda," the obnoxious one will beg, "save my Oo-La-La."

As Nurse Gina and I prepare to operate, I realise that what we really need here is some good old-fashioned alligator medicine.

So we call in Grandma Lou, who comes in with her alligator wrestling outfit on! And before you know it, she has pulled the alligator off the operating table and is in a wrestling ring with it. Ninky-Wink watches in horror as Grandma Lou has the alligator in a twisting leg hold. Gina Lash and I enjoy the show, eating popcorn and doggie treats..

Grandma Lou then delivers the final squeeze hold around the waist of the alligator and the poofy puffy little poodle flies right out of the alligator's mouth into Nanette's arms. Nanette and Oo-La-La land on the operating table, which shoots off down the hall. As it hits a wall, they fly out of the window into the swamp beyond where Ninnie-Poo is covered in mud.

"Don't fret, little Nin. You and Oo-La-La can live happily ever after!" And at that, Grandma Lou and I salute each other with bottles of soda pop. I take a slug and hear a burp.

I heard another burp, and, as I looked up at the table, I realised that it was coming from the teeny tiny baby creature that Grandma Lou was feeding with a baby bottle.

"That's right, drink your milk, Barney Boy," she was saying to it. "And when you grow up, you can chase that pesky Sheriff Boone off my property."

"That's Barney?" I said, as if I could not believe my eyes. And I could not, because he looked like he could hardly eat a fly, he was so tiny.

"Of course, Angel-wings," said my dad. "You didn't think they'd let Grandma bring a full-grown alligator on the plane, did you?"

But if that was Barney, who could not eat a fly, let alone a dog, where was Oo-La-La? As if she could read my mind, King started barking. And even though she is not good in obedience school, there are some things that King can do better than any other dog, and that is, she knows how to let me know what she wants to say.

"What is it girl?" I asked. "Oo-La-La's alive? Take me to him, girl!"

King ran out of the door with me following. And after chasing her down the street, and all over town, we found Oo-La-La stuck down a manhole in a sewer drain. It was so gross and stinky down there, but I didn't care, the important thing was to save Oo-La-La. And I never thought I'd say this, but was I ever glad to see that un-French French poodle!

Chapter 6

We brought him back to the Manoirs' house as soon as we could.

All Little Nin could say was, "See? I told you he would return home." I don't know who smelled worse from the drain pipe, me or Oo-La-La, but one thing is for sure, Nanette Manoir's manners stink.

"Ee-yew!" she said. "Angela Anaconda, excusez-moi, but you smell!"

Was that all she could think of to say to me after I had rescued her perfect little dog?

"Maybe you should try saying thank you," I said. But then I had a great idea. "Or KISSES." And at that, Oo-La-La, who had spent a lot more time in that sewer pipe than I had and who was covered in filthy sewage, jumped up on his perfect, baloney-headed owner and gave her a big wet kiss on the lips.

"Eew! Stop! Oo-La-La, stop!" gagged Ninky-Wink, as if she was going to throw up for real. And for once, Oo-La-La did not follow instructions, but kept kissing her and kissing her.

"Good trick, Oo-La-La," I said. "Good trick." And I meant it, too.

Story Number Two
Pet Peeves

Chapter 1

You might think that this story I am about to tell you has nothing to do with pets, but if you stay with it for a while, you will see that it does. It all started when I was excited to get to school (for once) because it was the day for our class to vote on where to go for our annual class trip.

Me and Johnny Abatti already knew what we were going to pick: the Monster Truck Rally! And I told Gordy Rhinehart that if he didn't vote for trucks, I'd tell Gina Lash not to marry him. So if Nanette Manoir, the pukey princess of Tapwater Springs told all of her friends to vote for opera-singing or

France, who cares? We would still have the most votes.

"Don't even start," said Gina Lash, as I met up with her on the way to school. "I'm voting for Mapperson's Bakery."

"If you vote for trucks, I'll give you my raspberry-flavoured lip gloss," I told her. And because Gina Lash cannot resist the temptation of something that tastes good that she can have right away, she all of a sudden decided that the Monster Truck Rally was a great idea for the class trip.

In the classroom we were all set as soon as Mrs Brinks called for suggestions for places to go on our annual field trip. I chose Johnny Abatti to suggest the Monster Truck Rally, on account of Mrs Brinks would never listen to a suggestion that was a suggestion from me. But before Johnny could say our excellent idea, we would have to hear the really bad idea that the teacher's pet rat, Nanette Manoir, suggested.

"The Ballet Russe is coming to perform Tchaikovsky's Swan Lake. I've arranged for sixteen tickets for us all to attend. They're throwing in a video documentary on the complete history of ballet shoes at no extra cost," she said, as if that was such a good thing.

I don't have to tell you that Nanette's clone drones, January and Karlene, were clapping like two trained seals in the zoo, but the rest of us just wanted to throw up in a throw-up bag. Then Mrs Brinks, acting as if this was the best and only idea in the entire world, wrote 'Ballet Russe' on the board and said, "What a wonderful and appropriate idea, Nanette. Now, class, if there are no other suggestions –"

I raised my hand. "Mrs Brinks! Mrs Brinks!" I called. "Johnny Abatti has another suggestion!"

And Johnny turned red like his head was going to blow up and he blurted out, "Monster Truck Rally."

At that, everybody who wasn't a Clone Club member jumped up and cheered out loud, so Mrs Brinks was forced to write 'Monster Truck Rally' on the board, even though she didn't want to. Then it was time to vote and, just like I knew we would, we won!

Then, because she is so good at cheating and dirty tricks, Nin the Pin raised her hand with a suggestion. "Since you'll be attending the field trip with us, Mrs Brinks," she said, "I certainly think that you should have a vote as well."

Instead of pointing out that she is not a student and not part of the class and not eligible to vote at all, Mrs Brinks said, "How thoughtful of you, Nanette, as always." And she put another tick against 'Ballet Russe'.

"There," she added. "It's a draw." Now what were we going to do? Too bad for us, Nanette Manoir had another bad idea.

"Since we students help fund-raise for field trips, perhaps the side that raises the most money should get to decide?"

"Why yes, of course, a fund-raising contest!" said Mrs Brinks. "Thank you, Nanette, for your resourceful and creative suggestion!"

And because of this creative and interesting suggestion, we now had to come up with a plan to make enough money to win the fund-raising contest, so that we could go to the Monster Truck Rally that most of us wanted to go to.

Chapter 2

Out in the playground, neither Johnny Abatti nor Gina Lash thought we had much of a chance.

"I knew I should have voted for Mapperson's Bakery," said Gina Lash. "Those Cinnamon Swirls, so hot and fresh and – "

"FREE!" I shouted, remembering that Mr Mapperson sometimes gave away free samples to people who visited the bakery. We would get Mr Mapperson to give us some free samples of baked goods and then we would sell them!

But a few hours later, when we had not sold one single thing at our 'Bakery Goods for Sale' stand, we figured our plan had not worked.

"How was I supposed to know Mapperson's Bakery wouldn't give away the good stuff?" asked Gina Lash.

"But Gina Lash," I said. "Stale wheat-free bread? Nobody buys that and I know this on account of we have been here selling it for more than two hours and not one person has bought a single slice."

Then, just when I thought things could not get any worse, they did, for who should ride by on her fancy un-French bike but Ninky-Wink herself. She held up a handful of money that she had just made from selling ballet shoe-shaped cookies.

"See you at the ballet, Angela! Au revoir!"

"Oh-revoir to you, Nannoying Nanette who's not really French Manoir! We've got lots of good ideas to make money, just you wait and see." All we had to do was think of them.

Chapter 3

It did not take long for us to come up with the best idea. We went into the garage to look for King, who is my best non-human friend in the world. She was asleep on the floor and my dad was busy with one of his inventions, a 'Bust-n-Blow', a sort of handheld hair dryer that blows out and sucks in air all at the same time.

Anyway, before I could ask him why he would invent such a thing, he said, "Shall we give her a whirl?" And he flicked the switch making the loudest noise you have ever heard. King jumped up and started barking, and the machine sucked in all this dust and fluff, then blew it all over the place. Not only was everything in the garage covered in dirt and fluff, but so was poor King.

My dad looked around and could not believe what a big mess he had made and before my mum could ask what was happening, he handed us some money.

"Here's five bucks. You guys go and clean up King and I'll clean up this mess." What did he say? For five dollars we would have cleaned up an elephant if he had wanted us to, and then, all of a sudden, Gina Lash, smartest in the class, came up with the best fund-raising idea: a pet wash for pets.

So in no time flat, we had everyone in Tapwater Springs who had a pet (which is just about everyone) lined up with their pets for us to wash them. Was this a great way to make money or what? And everything was going fine until Gordy

Rhinehart showed up with his little dog, Fabio, whose hair was so shaggy and long that neither Gina, Johnny nor I could tell where his head was.

"I think this calls for the Flo-bee," said Gina Lash in her expert way. Gina's mum only lets her use the Flo-bee trimmer on special occasions like holidays. And she usually uses it to shave the hair off her dolls that she is tired of. But looking at Fabio, I could only agree that he was in bad need of a haircut, even if Gordy Rhinehart didn't think so.

While Gina Lash was giving Fabio a much-needed trim, we heard the voice of a much un-needed, un-French person.

"Biscuits for sale! Get your _très_ delicious doggie biscuits, which I made myself, since I am so creative!" And there was Ninnie Wart selling her fancy dog biscuits with her pet dog, Oo-La-La, dressed in a tutu, making money at our fund-raiser!

Then Gordy Rhinehart almost fainted and had to breathe with his inhaler because Fabio, who was little to begin with, looked a lot smaller because all of his shaggy hair was gone and he was totally bald! I told Gordy that I'd rather have a rat with one head than a dog with two behinds and this made Fabio mad at me and he started growling.

They say bad things happen in threes and it must be true, because at the same time Dinky Nink was selling her biscuits to our customers and Fabio was getting his trim, Johnny Abatti was trying to wash Kitty Takanawa, Ms Jenerette the crossing guard's cat. Kitty Takanawa, who was scared of baths, had her claws in Johnny's head so he couldn't put her in the tub. She only jumped off when Fabio and all of the other dogs in the line (and there were a lot of them) started to chase her.

Kitty Takanawa ran up a tree and we told Johnny Abatti that since it was all his fault, he had to go up and get her down, even if he is afraid of heights. Meanwhile, all of the other dogs were loose in the yard, knocking over our washing tubs filled with water, making the yard one gigantic muddy puddle. Lucky for Johnny Abatti, a fireman came and saved him and got him down from the tree. Unlucky for us, that fireman bought the rest of Ninnie Wart's disgusting dog barf-scuits. All the

dogs we had washed were now dirty from the mud, and King was the muddiest one of all.

"Mud baths?" laughed Nanette, as she counted her money. "How continental, Angela Anaconda. Perhaps you'd like to be my escort to the Ballet Russe, John?"

Sometimes Johnny Abatti is too slow to think for himself, so it was up to me to squeeze between him and the Nan-evil one.

"How can he be your escort, if where we are going is the Monster Truck Rally?" I asked. "In case you don't know it, we made...Gina Lash?" Gina Lash had been adding up all the money we had collected.

"Eleven dollars and thirty-eight cents," she said. This only made Ninnie-Poo laugh more.

"In case you didn't

know," she said, as if she knew everything (which she does not), "unless your parents give you an extra three hundred and sixty-two dollars, which I most seriously doubt, I'm afraid you'll be doing something cultural for a change!"

What did she say? Even Gina Lash smartest in the class was amazed that this un-French Fry could make so much more money than us. And as if the sky knew how we were feeling, a huge thunder bolt made a crashing sound and it started to rain.

Nanette Manoir just opened up a little umbrella and said, "Coming, John?" and they left and I was steaming mad! As I watched them go, the sound of the thunder sounded just like the sound of thunderous clapping.

And I see Margot Fancy-Dancer Manoir and Johnny-Go-Lightly in their very tight ballet tights, escorting one another to Swan Lake. Since I am the orchestra conductor and am bored by ballet, I decide it is time to speed things up and get this show on the road! And as the music gets faster and faster, Johnny and Nanette are spinning faster and faster too. Too bad for Ninnie-Poo, Johnny seems to have lost his grip and she has spun right into the lake, where the Giant Swans with the faces of Mrs Brinks, January and Karlene are not only angry but ugly too.

"Angela! Angela!" you will cry. "Save me from the Swans who don't seem to know my head from my ballet shoes." But what a shame, Little Nin, the Swans are now bouncing you and your Prince Charmless back and forth on their beaks. Uh oh! There goes Johnny Abatti, up into a tree. Since he's so afraid of heights, I guess I will have no choice but to get into my fireman costume and come to the rescue.

"There you go, Johnny Back-stabber," I will tell him, as I bounce him back into the audience. But what's that? Little Nin cannot swim? Good thing she has on that tutu which holds her up in the water. Then I use my fireboat to pump all the water out of the lake leaving Ninky-Wink to roll around in the mud.

"Oh, Ninnie Poo," I will say. "You are covered in mud! How conti-numbskull! But fear not, Little Nin, this is ballet beauty mud. See how soft it makes your hair?" And just to prove my point, I take out my dad's new Bust-n-Blow and give it a blast. And now Ninnie's golden ringlets are hard as a rock. Thank goodness for Gina Lash's Flo-bee trimmers, because now I have you in the barber's chair so I can give you a nice new poodle cut.

"Cool in summer and you'll be the last person in our class to

catch lycee, which is French for 'lice'." But it's time to stop admiring yourself, Noodle-Poodle because we've got a Truck Rally to go to. I spin the chair round and you fly through the air. And what's that I see coming up to snack on your fuzzy pom-pom head? Why, it's the Robo-saurus!

"Angela! Angela! Help me! The Robo-Saurus wants to eat my puffy hair, like you so intelligently predicted, oh Angela, better fund-raiser than I," you will cry. But fear not, Pin Nin, I will hop aboard my Monster Truck and crash it into the Robo-Saurus, which makes it spit you out into the audience, right into the lap of your no-good escort, Johnny Abatti. There is thunderous clapping that turns to the sound of thunder.

Chapter 5

As I walk to school the next day in the pouring, thundering rain, I am soaked and my feet are covered in mud as I go in the door. Mrs Brinks, of course, is congratulating her pet creepy crêpe Nanette for winning the fund-raising competition hands down.

"Mrs Brinks! Someone has tracked mud all over our classroom and if it were me, which of course it is not, I would certainly volunteer to stay after class and clean it up," says guess who.

So that is how I ended my day, scrubbing the school floor. But if all good things come to an end, so do all bad things. At least my friends, Johnny Abatti and Gina Lash waited for me so we all could walk home together.

"Think they'll have real swans at Swan Lake?" asked Johnny.

"Maybe one will go crazy and attack Mrs Brinks and Nanette," I said. "That'd be almost as good as the Robo-Saurus."

"You guys are making me hungry," said Gina Lash. "Anyone for Mapperson's Bakery?"

"For wheat free bread, Gina Lash?" I asked.

"No," said Gina, licking her lips. "For eleven dollars and thirty-eight cents worth of Cinnamon Swirls!"

Turtle Confessions

Chapter 1

I don't know about you, but when I do something I feel ashamed of, I need to tell someone all about it. And because it is something I am ashamed of, the only person I tell is Josephine Praline, who will sit in a box with you, listen to your confession and then not tell anyone what you told her, not anyone!

I don't know how or why she does it, but I am really glad that she does. And on this day I am going to tell you about, I had to talk to Josephine Praline really badly. So badly that I even forgot about playing tetherball, which is the only part of the school day that is my favourite part.

"Now then, Angela Anaconda," said Josephine. "Start from the beginning and take your time. But not too much time. There's a heavenly game of tetherball going on and Candy May is being an angel and saving me a place."

So then I took a deep breath and tried to get the courage to tell Josephine Praline about the horrible thing that I had done.

"It all began when Gina Lash's mother decided to take her to Club Carumba for the weekend and Gina Lash didn't know who to leave Sheldon, her pet turtle, with," I started telling Josephine. So far so good. Then I told her how Gordy Rhinehart really wanted to mind Sheldon and not just because he is in love with Gina Lash.

"Most people find turtles boring to play with," he told Gina Lash. "But I relate to their shy, skittish natures."

And all of a sudden I got very jealous, as in who is your best friend anyway Gina Lash, him or me? And even though I don't really need any more pets, I really wanted to make Gina Lash pick me to mind Sheldon. I even offered to give her my two-headed nickel from my mutant coin collection.

"Hey! That's bribery!" yelled Gordy Rhinehart.

"Gordy's right," said Gina Lash. "I have to make my decision based on what's best for Sheldon." Then Gordy Rhinehart showed Gina Lash a little turtle neck sweater that he had knitted for Sheldon. Now who was bribing? So then, I had to pull out my most secret weapon, my dad's field handbook of turtles and tortoises.

If you know anything about Gina Lash, there are two ways to her heart: one is with food (especially Tiny Dottie Cakes or Mapperson Bakery Cinnamon Swirls), the other is with books. Even though I had never even opened this handbook and knew nothing about what it said, Gina Lash was very impressed.

"Wow!" she said. "A 1964 edition of Lengensheidt's *Schildrote Kleinhandbuch*! When it comes to turtles, he's tops! Now I really can't decide who to leave Sheldon with!" Gordy Rhinehart was giving me a very dirty look. I never realised he was so competitive. It made me want to mind Sheldon even more. That's when I pulled out my other secret weapon.

"I know, Gina Lash," I said. "Why don't we flip for it?"

"Well, I wouldn't normally leave anything as important as Sheldon's well-being to a flip of the coin, but since time is of the essence..." Gina said, as she threw my coin in the air. "Call it, Angela Anaconda!"

Now, I knew it was wrong, but I really, really wanted to

take care of Sheldon for the weekend. The coin we were using was the two-headed one from my mutant coin collection, so as long as I called "heads" I could not lose.

"Heads," I said. Even Josephine Praline seemed shocked when I was telling her this.

"Holy mother of pearl! You tricked your own best friend?" she asked.

But tricking Gina Lash and Gordy Rhinehart with a two-headed coin was not the thing that was bothering me. It was all the stuff that happened later!

Chapter 2

I watched Gina Lash and her mother drive away for the weekend with Sheldon in my hands. My dream had come true. But now the question was, what was I going to do with Sheldon? Have you ever tried playing with a turtle? I mean, what fun are they anyway? I tried throwing a ball for him to fetch, but he just sat there. I tried to teach him to roll over, but he just sat there. I taped a ping pong bat to his back and put him on the table, thinking he might like that, but he wouldn't even play ping pong and that is a very fun game.

To tell you the truth, Sheldon was the most boring pet in the world and I had to mind him the whole weekend! Thank goodness I heard Johnny Abatti yelling for me. I looked out of my window and he was standing there in his flippers and a scuba mask.

"My Uncle Nicky installed the Aqua Pronto computer-operated sprinkler system over at Nonna's," Johnny said. "Wanna go play?"

Did I ever! But then I remembered one very boring thing.

"Oh, I've got to be back in two hours to feed Gina Lash's do-nothing turtle like I have unfortunately promised I will," I said. If you know anything about playing in the Aqua Pronto sprinkler, then you know that two hours fly by as if they are nothing. You really need like ten hours to fully enjoy yourself. Then Johnny Abatti had a great idea, which is pretty amazing considering all the times he has been hit on the head with a hockey puck.

"Why don't you just feed him extra now, so you won't have to feed him later?" he asked. And since I did have a whole entire bag of mini-carrots and since Sheldon was just sitting in his terrarium waiting to be fed,

all I had to do was pour the entire bag in and I was free to enjoy endless hours of fun, jumping in the Aqua Pronto sprinkler system with Johnny Abatti. That is, until Gordy Rhinehart came along.

"Angela!" he yelled at me, as I was just in the middle of finally having some fun, getting soaking wet. "What are you doing? Isn't it time to feed Sheldon?"

"Relax, Gordy," I said. "Sheldon has enough food to last him at least the rest of his boring life, on account of I gave him extra." But instead of calming down and joining in the fun, which is what anyone else would have done, Gordy got all upset and excited.

"You did what?" he asked, as if he did not believe me.

"It was my idea," said Johnny Abatti, all proud of himself.

"But, Angela," said Gordy, still not calming down one bit. "If you over-feed a turtle, it will

59

eat itself to death!"

"Aw, c'mon, Gordy," I said. "If Gina Lash has never eaten herself to death, I don't think her pet turtle will."

"Yeah, relax," laughed Johnny Abatti. "Come and have some fun." Then he soaked Gordy with the water from the sprinkler and Gordy yelled at us and ran away.

CHAPTER 3

We had more hours of fun playing under the sprinkler and I only thought a little bit about what Gordy Rhinehart had said about over-feeding Sheldon. That is, until I got home. When I looked in Sheldon's terrarium he was gone! Johnny Abatti, who had come with me, couldn't find Sheldon either.

"Where do you think he's gone, Johnny Abatti?"

"I don't know. Maybe he's looking for a place to kick the bucket," said Johnny. "Once on 'National Explorer' they said that some animals leave their homes to find a good place to croak." What did he say? Could it be that Gordy was right? Could I have really fed Sheldon too much and now he was out there looking for somewhere to die? Johnny Abatti did not think this was as big a deal as I did. Probably because he does not have any pets. (That is, unless you count the rats that run around the kitchen of Abatti's Pizza or Sir Ducksworthy, his sock puppet.)

"At least Gina Lash will be glad that Sheldon went out with a full stomach," said Johnny, as if that made everything all right. But being Gina Lash's best friend, I knew how much Sheldon meant to her, even if he was just a boring turtle. The only thing that I could think of doing was finding a replacement for Sheldon and fast!

Chapter 4

First I called the Golden Shell Chinese Restaurant for an order of ginger Turtle soup.

"But hold the soup and the ginger. Just give me the turtle and don't cook him, please." For some reason they just hung up on me. Then, all I could think of was to actually go out and buy a Sheldon lookalike. In order to do this, I had to sell my prized mutant coin collection, which was the possession I most prized in the world, to my idiotic older brothers. But I had to do what I had to do, so I could go to the pet store with a picture of Sheldon and buy a turtle that looked just like him. The only question was, would this fool Gina Lash, smartest in the class?

Chapter 5

"**W**ow! Sheldon sure is peppy," is all Gina Lash said, when she returned from Club Carumba, as the new turtle tried to squirm away from her. She never even suspected.

"Shame on you, Angela Anaconda!" Josephine Praline, said as I was telling her all this.

"I know," I agreed with her. "I tricked and lied to my best friend, Gina Lash." Then Josephine Praline said something that I had never really thought about.

"Forget about Gina. What about poor Sheldon?" She asked. "Put yourself in his shell. Think of the horrors that helpless turtle went through before his untimely end."

What did she say? And it was true. I never did think about Sheldon on account of the fact that he was no fun and a boring pet that did nothing. But now I sure was thinking about him and I realised that I was even a worse person than I thought I was! I wanted to keep talking to Josephine about what I should do, but it was her turn to be up for tetherball.

"Wait, Josephine!" I called. If she left to play tetherball, then who else could I talk to? I tried to follow her out of the confession box we had been sitting in, but the box got stuck on my head and I banged into a tree.

As I lay on the ground in the dark I thought, "I wonder if this is what Josephine meant about putting myself in Sheldon's shell, because I sure feel like Sheldon now."

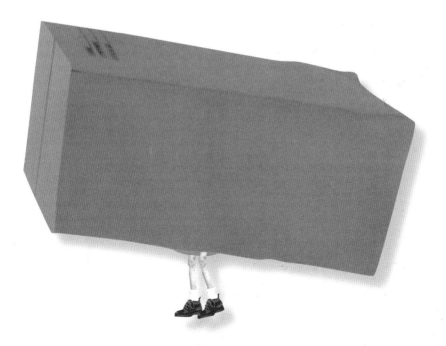

And before I knew it, I was in a turtle shell in a turtle terrarium. My mother always told me to come out of my shell, but now that I am in one, I don't think it's such a good idea because giant carrots are raining down on my head.

"Help me! Help me!" I will cry. "Save me from this mega-downpour of mini-carrots!" And I meant it, too. Then a giant hand reaches into the terrarium and instead of being terrified, I am happy.

"Hooray! It is Gordy Rhinehart, friend to turtles," I say as Gordy puts one of his hand-knitted sweaters on me. I am glad that Gordy is trying to keep me warm, but soon I am too hot in my matching little turtle hat, scarf and mittens.

"Don't worry, little turtle," Gordy will tell me. "Nonna's Aqua Pronto will cool you off." And we are outside and the sprinkling system comes on, but because I am a little turtle, I am rocketed up in the air by the water pressure. Then my sweater, scarf, hat and mittens all begin to shrink.

"Uh-oh," I say. "This shrinking sweater is shrinking and making me think that maybe I am too big to be a tiny turtle."

Just then another giant hand picks me up. It is none other than Nonna Abatti and she is very happy with a new idea that she just loves.

"Nicky! Nicky!" she calls. "Come here and look! I gotta great idea for a new pizza, huh? Turtle pizza!"

And as Nonna sets to work with her rolling pin, I am calling and begging, but I am too small for anyone to hear me, "No! Please! I'm too young to be a topping!"

Chapter 6

As I am cowering and shaking, bright sunshine floods in. The top of my box has been opened and there, looking in at me are Gina Lash, with the squirmy new turtle that she still thinks is Sheldon, and Gordy Rhinehart.

"Angela! We've been looking all over for you," said Gina Lash. "We were just playing with Sheldon, when we noticed!"

The moment of truth had come. If there was nothing left I could do for Sheldon, at least I could tell Gina Lash the whole horrible truth.

"That's not Sheldon!" I said.

"What?" asked Gina Lash, as if she did not understand one word. I spoke as quickly as I could. I had to get this over with and Gina Lash had to know the truth. It was the least I could do.

"Gina Lash, I have something terrible to tell you. Sheldon

bought the turtle farm and it's all my fault on account of I fed him too much food for a turtle to eat. So I got you a new turtle and just told you it was Sheldon. But he's not really Sheldon, seeing as he's another different turtle completely!" There! I had said it.

"I know, Angela Anaconda," said Gina Lash. "And I've decided to call him Zippy. This is Sheldon." And she held up not one, but two turtles! But how in the world could this be, after I did such a bad and terrible job minding him?

"It was me, Angela Anaconda," said Gordy Rhinehart. "I

was worried for Sheldon's well-being, so I kidnapped him while you and Johnny Abatti were playing in the sprinkler. I took care of him myself."

"You knew all along and you didn't tell me?" I asked Gina Lash.

"I figured it could wait," she said. "Especially since you were too busy playing with Josephine."

"Playing? I was confessing!" I said. And even though telling the truth about what I did had made me feel better, the fact that Sheldon was alive and well made me feel great.

"Anyone for turtle races?" asked Gina Lash. Now that she has two turtles, I guess we had a new game to play.

STORY NUMBER FOUR
PUPPY Love

Chapter 1

There are days when you see things you wish you had not and days when you wish you could see things that you cannot and today I, Angela Anaconda, am going to tell you about the day I had both of these things. It was the day that Mr and Mrs Brinks opened their pool for the summer. Me and my friends, Johnny Abatti, Gina Lash and Gordy Rhinehart, were all up in our tree-house with binoculars and instant cameras, hoping to get proof of what we already knew – that our teacher Mrs Brinks and her husband are both nudists, who walk around their house with no clothes on, nude.

"I think we should eat the cupcakes I brought right now," said Gina Lash, "'cause the sight of the Brinkses naked might make us lose our appetites."

"I brought allergy-free rice crackers for everyone," said Gordy Rhinehart. "They always settle my stomach."

"Shhh!" I said, not because I saw something, but because I heard something. Johnny Abatti and I stopped trying to look into the Brinks's yard and leaned out of the tree-house into my yard instead. Then I saw the first thing that I wished I had not seen. Nanette Manoir, my most hated enemy in the world, was in my yard with her gardener, Alfredo, and he was hammering something into our tree!

"What are you doing here?" I asked. "And why is your

gardener attacking our tree?"

"For your information, Angela Anaconda, he is putting up a *très* important community notice," said the snot-nosed one. But in the next second she started to cry. "My valuable, pure-bred French poodle, Oo-La-La, has gone missing!"

"Nanette, don't cry," said Johnny Abatti, because he is too nice for his own good. "We'll help you find him." This called for a group meeting. Ninky-Wink was distracting us from our mission.

"We've got special business to do first," I reminded my friends. "Remember Operation Beached Whale?" At that, we heard what we had been waiting for all morning, the sound of blubber hitting the water at the Brinkses.

"Come on, Angela," said Johnny. "What if your dog was missing?"

"My dog wouldn't run away," I said.

"My dog is loyal." And I meant it too. There is not another dog more friendly, honest and loyal than good old King, my best non-human friend in all the world.

"By the way," called the horrible one on her way out of my yard. "My father is offering a two hundred dollar reward for whoever finds my Oo-La-La."

What did she say? Two hundred dollars as in one hundred weeks allowance times two? We were out of the tree-house in no time!

"Come on, doggie. Where are you?" called Johnny Abatti.

"Here, doggie, doggie," wheezed Gordy. Even Gina Lash forgot all about her cupcakes.

"Let's go and find that poodle," she said to me.

"I guess the Brinkses will still be naked tomorrow," I said. And even though I was a little disappointed not to carry out our original plan, I was looking forward to collecting that two hundred dollar reward.

CHAPTER 2

After spending the entire day doing something as boring as looking for a yappy little dog, we all met up back in the tree-house.

"What a waste of a day!" I said.

"No reward money and no bare Brinkses!" agreed Gina Lash.

"And all because of Nanette 'ruin-our-day' Manoir," I said. And I really meant it. It was so late, it was time to go home. Can you imagine not having fun for one whole entire day off from school? I was still thinking about how we had ruined our whole day, when I saw something that I could not believe I was seeing. Right there in my own backyard, sitting with King, was Oo-La-La! My day was not wasted after all, and not only that, I would soon be rich.

"C'mon, Oo-La-Blah," I said, as I tried to pull him out of our yard. "I want my two hundred dollars and you want to go home, right?" But instead of coming with me, that little yippy pet of a teacher's pet growled and snapped at me. Oo-La-La did not want to leave King and go home to his creepy un-French owner. I couldn't blame him for that, but still I wanted my reward money.

I tried speaking some un-French French. I tried playing with a rope. I tried being nice. I tried being mean. Nothing worked. Oo-La-La would not budge.

"Fine," I finally said. "Stay here with King if King can stand it. I'll go and get your unfortunate owner." With that, I marched off to the Manoirs to get Ninnie-Poo herself.

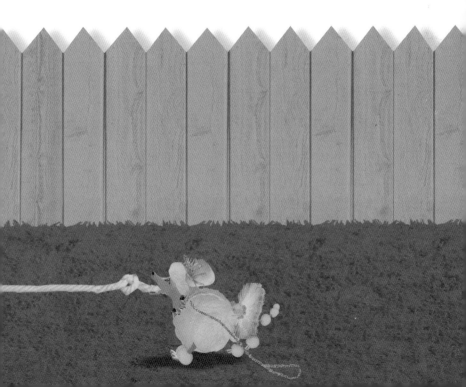

Chapter 3

Now if you know anything about me, you would know that nothing in the world can make me go over to Nanette Manoir's house. But number one, I was getting her to get her poofy little dog out of my yard, and number two, I was going to collect a big reward for finding him. I would soon have more money than I ever saw in my entire life. So, as you can imagine, I was sort of in a hurry to ring the doorbell and get this all over with. But Little Nin, being her pain in the neck self, was not about to make this easy. Mainly, she did not believe me when I told her that her dog was over at my house.

"Oh please, my dog would sooner visit the city dump than visit your house. Not that there's much distinction," said her monstrous face over the front door monitor. (Nanette Manoir is not like a normal person who comes to the door to speak to you when you go to her house. Instead, she speaks over an intercom monitor and you have to look at her big baloney-headed face on a little TV screen.)

In order to remind myself why I should try to be patient with the Royal Nin and not scream at her, I kept repeating to myself, "Two hundred dollars, two hundred dollars."

"I heard that!" screeched Na-nincompoop. "You should be ashamed of yourself, Angela Anaconda. Showing up here trying to cheat me out of the reward, while my poor Oo-La-La's still out there somewhere, lost and alone." What did she say? No matter how much I tried to convince her to come with me to see for herself, Nin the Pin just would not believe me. I finally left when she threatened to call Security. I just needed proof that Oo-La-La was really in my yard. And with Johnny Abatti's instant camera, which develops the pictures instantly, I would show Nanette Manoir, once and for all.

CHapter 4

In no time at all, I had all of my friends back in my yard. So now, instead of spying on a pair of naked Brinkses, we were spying on King and Oo-La-La. And to tell you the truth, I don't know which was more embarrassing. I mean, King was snuggling up to that puny little un-French French poodle, Oo-La-La, as if she were in love with him. Yech! What was she thinking? Another horrible thing I had to see that day.

"Well, what are you waiting for, Johnny Abatti? Start

snapping!" I said. Then Johnny Abatti took the whole role of film, just to make sure we got some good pictures.

"I wonder what Nanette will say when she sees these," I said, because these pictures were perfect proof that the truth I had been trying to tell her before was true. And for the second time that day I was in a hurry to get to Ninky-Winky's ugly house. When she heard that I had photographic evidence, she let me in. But things never seem to work out the way that you think they are going to, especially when it comes to Nanette. When she looked at the pictures she started screaming and all her screaming brought in her mum and dad, who think she is the best thing in all the world.

"What is it, Princess?" begged her father.

"Yes, tell Mummy and Daddy," said her mother, who had to fan Nanette to keep her from fainting.

Instead of saying, "Angela Anaconda found my lost dog and we should give her the reward money right away" like she should have said, Nitzy Ditz stood up and pointed her finger at me and started yelling again.

"She dog-napped my poodle and now she's trying to

blackmail me!" she said. And the worst thing is, her parents are just like our teacher Mrs Brinks, believing that anything that comes out of little pet Ninnygoat's mouth is perfect and true! They looked at the instant pictures that Johnny Abatti had taken instantly, as if they proved that I had stolen Oo-La-La!

"But I wasn't blackmailing," I said. "I don't even know what that means!" And it is true, I still don't know. "I found your dog! I only took the photos so that you would believe me!"

"Oh Mummy, Daddy, now she's calling me a liar!" cried Nanette and she started sobbing so much that even I almost felt sorry for her! Her parents were besides themselves, trying to get her to stop crying.

"Tell Mummy how to make her little Peach feel better," said her mum.

"Anything," said her dad and he meant it.

"Oh, I don't need anything," sighed Nin. "Maybe you could donate the reward money to my favourite charity." Then her father said something even worse.

"That's my precious. Always putting others first." Huh?

"Wouldn't you rather have that pretty little frock we saw in window of Marcel's Boutique?" asked her mum.

"Say!" said her dad, as if this were the greatest idea on earth. "We could use the reward money to buy it for you!" And of course Nanette agreed, and in no time at all, she was happy again.

"And don't forget to send someone to rescue my poor, precious Oo-La-La," she said.

"Alfredo!" called her mum, because she does anything that Nanette wants. "To the Anacondas! Chop! Chop! And be sure to bring plenty of doggy disinfectant with you!"

Chapter 5

You might have thought that storming out of there without one cent of the reward money, which I so very much deserved, was the worst part of my day. But it was not. Not by a long shot. The worst part of my day happened after I got home. After Alfredo drove off with Oo-La-La in the Manoir's Town Car, my King started whimpering as she watched him go, as if she was sad.

"Look on the bright side, girl," I said, glad to be rid of that yippy little mutt. "You won't have to hang out with that snobby dog any more." And instead of feeling better, King started crying and running after the Manoirs' car! For the millioneth time that day, I could not believe my eyes!

"Come back! Wait! King!" I shouted, as I chased after her. And where do you think we ended up? Right at the driveway gates of the Manoirs' house! King raced in before the gates closed. Leaving me outside! And that was that. King had decided to stay with the Manoirs and leave me for ever! What could be worse than that?

Looking through those gates, I started thinking about how much I loved King and how I would never see her again.

Even when I am a little old lady, I will go through my photo albums and remember when we first met and how it was love at first sight. I will look at pictures of you, King, as a little puppy and think about all the fun we had when I was a little girl, like when we used to play tug-of-war. But, as I am going through these photos, a vision straight out of a nightmare appears.

"Hey, what's she doing here?" I will ask myself, as I see Nanette Manoir with her two hundred dollar dress on. Then, before you know it, Nanette is on one end of a tug-of-war rope, I am on the other and King is in the middle!

"Get lost, Ninnie-Poo! We don't want to play with you!" I will

tell her. And we will tug back and forth, back and forth, back and forth, until the rope breaks. And I fly off to one side and Ninky-Wink and King will fly off to the other. And as I look up to see that they are together and I am alone, I hear sad, sappy music like you hear in sad, sappy love movies.

"Maybe it's better this way, my former best friend," I say about King. "All I want is for you to be happy," is all I can say because I am almost crying. And King, Nanette and Oo-La-La go off into the sunset and the sappy music fills my eardrums.

"Even if it's not with me," I cry. And I mean it, too. I love King that much.

Chapter 6

And then, as I looked through those gates at that horrible house, which I never want to see again, all I could think about was how much I wanted to say one last goodbye to King. So I climbed over the gates and peeked in the window and, sure enough, there was my girl, sitting on a fancy cushion in the living-room next to her new love, Oo-La-La.

I could hear Ninny, happy as can be, coming down the hall. (Who wouldn't be happy to have King as their dog?)

"Oo-La-La, dear, to celebrate your return, I had Cook whip up your favourite – a cheese and asparagus soufflé. Made with Roquefort. That's French for –"

"Cheese that smells like shoes," I said to myself. But if that was how King wanted to live from now on, I would have to accept it. "Bye, King, it was great knowing you, girl," I said very quietly.

Then I saw Ninky walk into the room with her soufflé on a crystal plate and I guess she was surprised to see King there, because she dropped the plate and started to scream.

"Aah! What are you doing here? Mummy! Daddy! That mangy mutt is in my house!" And, as she was having her shrieking fit, King walked up to the soufflé, which had been spilled all over the floor, took one whiff of it and walked away. Ooh-La-La, on the other hand, loved it and started eating it all up. This made Nanette Manoir even crazier.

"No! No! No! Eating off the floor?" Then she gave King a horrible, mean Nan-nasty look. "He learned this from you, you insufferable mongrel!"

93

As she tried to pull Oo-La-La away from the food, he snarled at her and this made her scream even more. I could see that King had had enough of this place.

"King!" I called. And she looked up and jumped out of the window, right into my arms.

"You've come back!" I yelled because I was so happy. "C'mon girl, let's go home!" And I don't know which one of us was more excited to get out of there. All I know is we have lived happily ever after ever since!

THE END

"Hi, if you've enjoyed this book, why not read some more books about me, Angela Anaconda, and the other folks at Tapwater Springs. We have a cool selection."